This LazyTown Annual belongs to

....

Contents

Miss Roberta	8
Dancing in the Dark	16
Candy! Candy! Candy!	17
Colour it!	18
Move it!	20
Back of the Net	22
Rockin' Robbie	24
What's New, Pixel?	32
Step to the Beat!	34
The Colour of Rotten	36
Defeeted	38
Lazy Puzzles	46
Missing Melody	47
Let's Dance	48
Blow-up!	50
Rotten Potion	52
The Haunted Castle	54
Pick a Pose	62
Say Cheese!	63
Missing Links	64
The Big Quiz	66
Answers	68

EGMONT

We bring stories to life

First published in Great Britain 2008 by Egmont UK Limited
239 Kensington High Street, London W8 6SA
Created for Egmont by John Brown Publishing Group
Edited by William Petty • Designed by Grant Kempster
LazyTown © and ™ 2008 LazyTown Entertainment.
All related titles, logos and characters are trademarks of LazyTown Entertainment.
© 2008 LazyTown Entertainment. All rights reserved.

ISBN 978 1 4052 3906 6
1 3 5 7 9 10 8 6 4 2
Printed in Italy

Miss Roberta

"Come on Ziggy, you can do it!" laughed Trixie. Ziggy took a huge mouthful of fizzy drink ... and let out a huge burp!

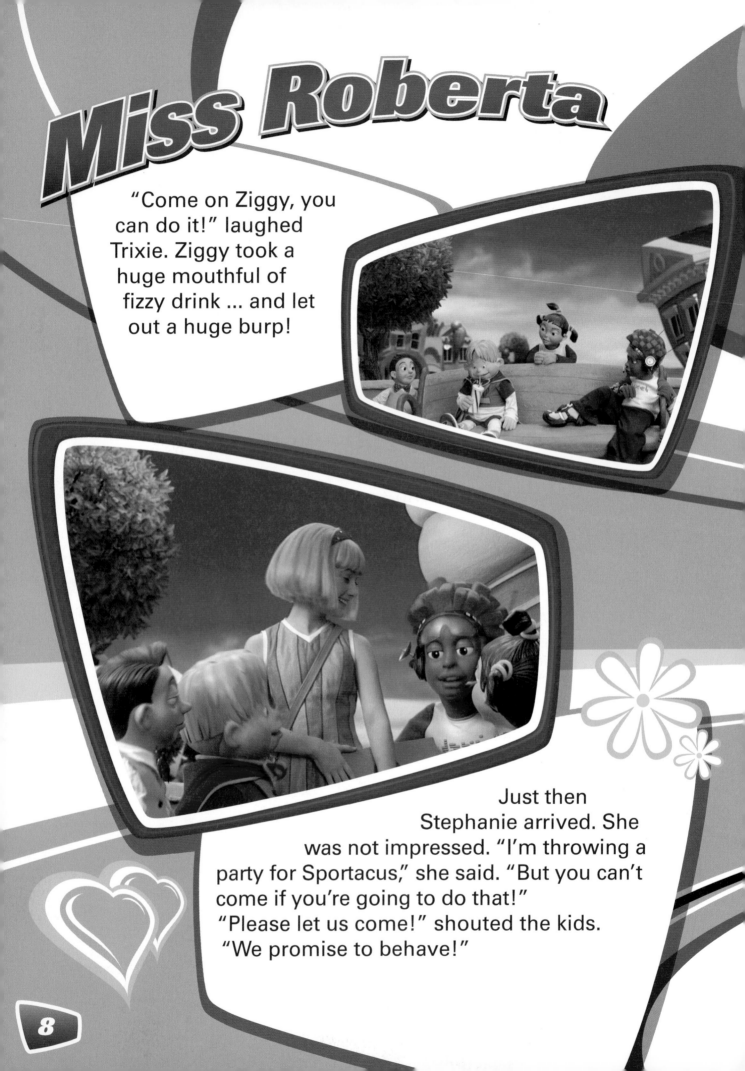

Just then Stephanie arrived. She was not impressed. "I'm throwing a party for Sportacus," she said. "But you can't come if you're going to do that!"
"Please let us come!" shouted the kids.
"We promise to behave!"

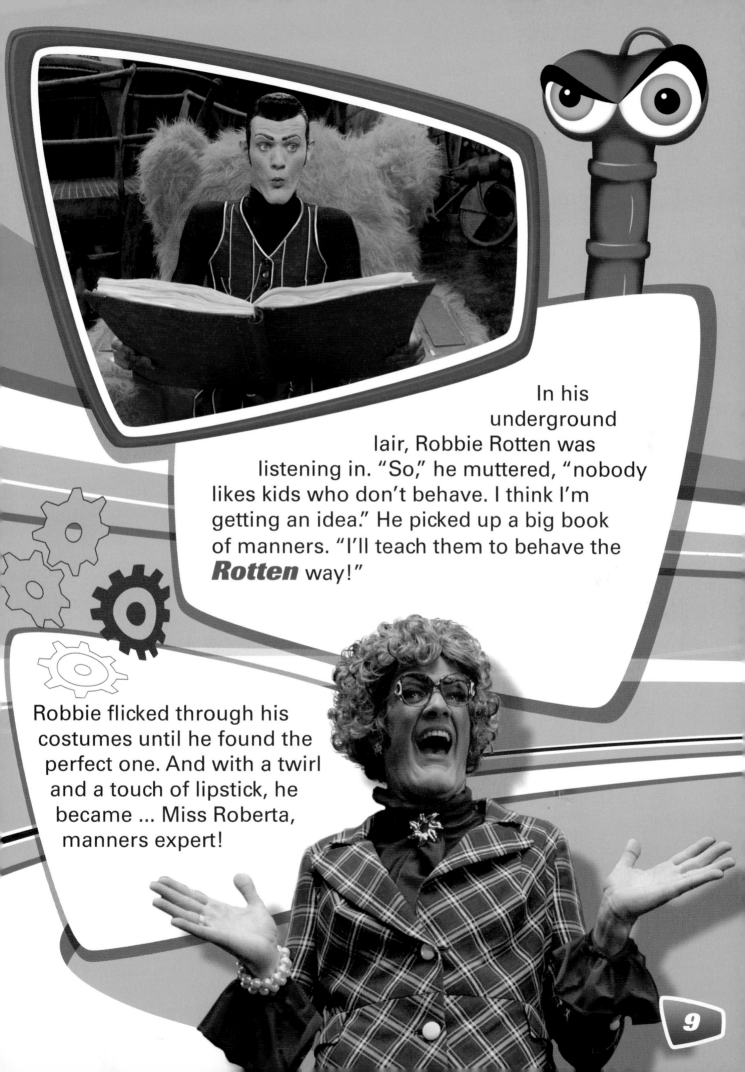

In his underground lair, Robbie Rotten was listening in. "So," he muttered, "nobody likes kids who don't behave. I think I'm getting an idea." He picked up a big book of manners. "I'll teach them to behave the **Rotten** way!"

Robbie flicked through his costumes until he found the perfect one. And with a twirl and a touch of lipstick, he became ... Miss Roberta, manners expert!

Meanwhile, the kids were baking a special cake for Sportacus. As they happily worked together, they heard a call from outside: "Learn manners here!"

Heading outside, the kids found a lady with a big book. "Did you say you can teach us manners?" asked Stephanie.

"You've come to the right place!" answered the lady. "I'm Miss Roberta, and when it comes to manners, I wrote the book." She patted the big book in her hands.

"Oh, thank you!" said Stephanie. "I'm having a party, and I was worried my friends would spoil it by behaving badly. Now I can relax." She then skipped off to practise her dancing.

Miss Roberta
began her
lesson.
"Now Ziggy,
you should burp
more. That's good manners.
And Stingy, it's polite to open
other people's presents
for them," she said.

When it was party time,
Stephanie went to find
Sportacus. "Come with me,
I have a surprise!" she said.
She opened the door to her
house, and found ...

... a complete mess! Ziggy had eaten half the cake, Stingy had opened all the presents, and Trixie was throwing streamers around.

"How could you do this?" cried Stephanie.
"Miss Roberta told us to!" replied the kids. "She told us it was good manners! And she's the expert!"

Stephanie turned to speak to Miss Roberta, but she had jumped out of the window. As Sportacus rushed outside, Miss Roberta tripped over a wheelbarrow.

Sportacus caught her as she fell, but as she did, her wig came off. "Robbie Rotten!" everyone cried. Robbie scuttled off, scowling.

"We're sorry, Sportacus!" said the kids. "We messed up the party."

"That's OK!" replied Sportacus. "You gave me something more important – your friendship!"

Back in his lair, Robbie eased his feet into a bowl of hot water. "Argh, those high heels!" he moaned. "My feet are so sore!"

Dancing in the Dark

Stephanie loves to touch her toes!
Can you find the shadow that
matches the picture?

a

b

c

d

e

f

Write it in!

Candy! Candy! Candy!

Ziggy's trying hard not to eat too much candy! Which path should he take to eat the carrot instead?

1

2

3

Write it in!

17

Answers on page 68

Colour it!

Colour in this big picture of the LazyTown gang, using the small picture as a guide!

18

Move it!

The little things you do every day don't have to be boring. Why not try doing them Sportacus-style? Then you'll be having fun in no time!

1

Spring out of bed every morning – jump as high as you can!

2

Flick on the light switch by stretching Sportacus-style!

Sportacus' *tip*

Move like Sportacus at least once a day, and you'll feel on top of the world!

4 Don't always walk – sometimes run! Lift your knees high and get there in half the time!

3 Don't bend your back to pick things up – bend your knees!

Back of the Net

Candy Candy

Anyone Can Be a Hero!

TRIXIE
LAZYTOWN F.C.

ROBOT 6
ROTTEN ROVERS

ROBOT 3
ROTTEN ROVERS

ZIGGY
LAZYTOWN F.C.

Start Here!

ROBOT 5
ROTTEN ROVERS

PIXEL
LAZYTOWN F.C.

Oh My Stars!

Let's Do... Nothing!

Which 2 robots are exactly the same?

Sportacus' tip

Use a ruler to see who you can pass to!

Get the ball here, then shoot for goal!

ROTTEN ROVERS · ROBOT 2

LAZYTOWN F.C. · SPORTACUS

ROTTEN ROVERS · ROBOT 4

LAZYTOWN F.C. · STEPHANIE

ROTTEN ROVERS · ROBOT 1

Where Do You Plug it In?

Believe in Yourself!

You Can Make It!

Hold On, I Have Another Call.

Answer on page 68

23

Rockin' Robbie

"Swing to the beat, and you're the king of the town." The LazyTown kids were having a band practice in the theatre. *"Sweet, sweet music, makes you feel so fine!"* Stingy sang, at the top of his voice.

Down in his lair, Robbie Rotten was woken up by the noise – and fell off his chair! "What is that **awful** racket?" he grumbled.

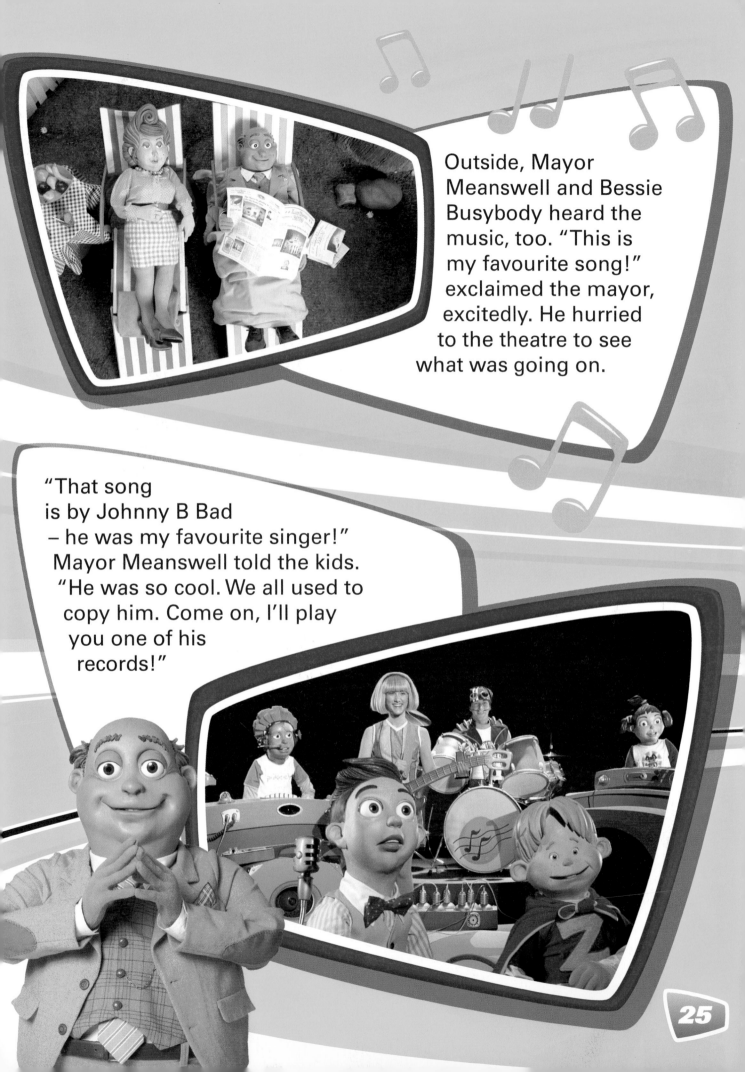

Outside, Mayor Meanswell and Bessie Busybody heard the music, too. "This is my favourite song!" exclaimed the mayor, excitedly. He hurried to the theatre to see what was going on.

"That song is by Johnny B Bad – he was my favourite singer!" Mayor Meanswell told the kids. "He was so cool. We all used to copy him. Come on, I'll play you one of his records!"

Back at his house, the mayor put on a record. The kids loved it! "I wish we could hear Johnny sing in person!" said Stephanie. "Then let's invite him to sing here, and give him a trophy!" said Mayor Meanswell.

Robbie was listening in, and getting an idea. "So, they want to give Johnny B Bad a trophy?" he muttered. "Then maybe he'll pay them a visit!" One quick change later, and Robbie was ready to rock and roll.

Meanwhile, Mayor Meanswell was about to call his hero. "I'm so nervous!" he said, as he dialled. "Hello? Is that Johnny B Bad?" he said.

But Robbie had switched the phone lines. "Yeah baby, that's me!" he said. "You want me to come and sing for you, and you're going to give me a trophy? Sure, I'll come to LazyTown!"

Later that day, Mayor Meanswell walked into his office – and found Robbie, in disguise, waiting for him. "Johnny B Bad!" the mayor exclaimed. "Would you come and say hello to the children? They're so excited!"

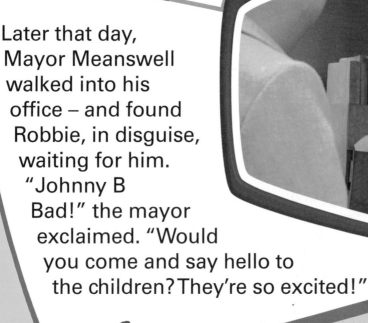

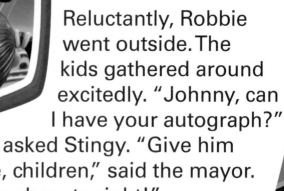

Reluctantly, Robbie went outside. The kids gathered around excitedly. "Johnny, can I have your autograph?" asked Stingy. "Give him some space, children," said the mayor. "He has a big show tonight!"

That evening,
Mayor Meanswell
knocked on Robbie's dressing
room door. The mayor had dressed up
specially just like Johnny. "Is there anything
you need?" he asked. "Yeah, there is one
thing," answered Robbie.
"Make sure Sportacus
doesn't come to
the concert."

The mayor
didn't want
to argue with
Johnny. Sadly,
he wrote a note to
Sportacus, asking him not to
come. Meanwhile, in the theatre,
the kids couldn't wait for the show
to begin.

Robbie hit play on a tape recorder and ran onstage. The crowd went wild as he sang one of 'his' hits. But halfway through the song, the tape stopped!

Robbie grabbed the trophy, and tried to run off. But at that moment, Sportacus arrived. Robbie tripped over his flares and his wig came off. The crowd gasped. "It's Robbie Rotten!" they cried.

Robbie ran away.
"At least Robbie didn't
get the trophy," said Sportacus.
"But we still need a concert," said
Stephanie. "Luckily we've been
practising. Let's play!"

Back in his lair, Robbie
had to listen to the
concert. "That was the
stupidest thing I've ever
done," he groaned. Then
he knocked a piece of
cake into his lap. "No,
that was the stupidest
thing I've ever
done!"

These pictures look the same, but 10 things are different in picture 2. Can you spot them all?

What's New, Pixel?

1

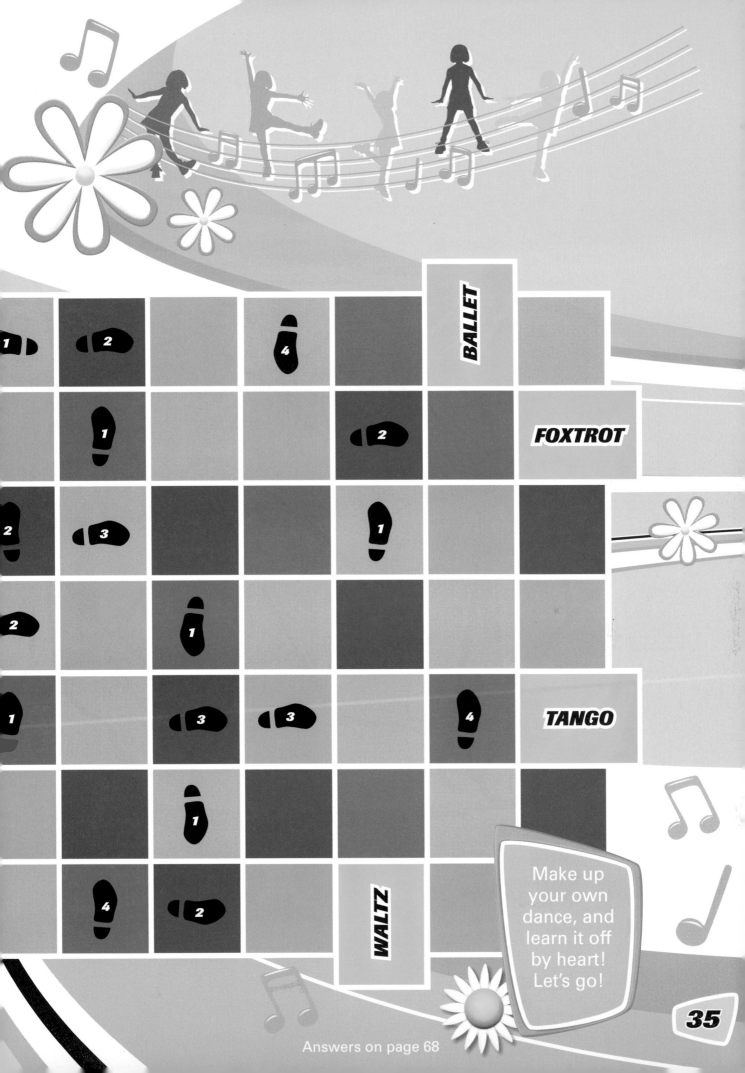

BALLET

FOXTROT

TANGO

WALTZ

Make up your own dance, and learn it off by heart! Let's go!

The Colour of Rotten

It's all gone wrong for Robbie – again! Use this code to colour in him and 'that pink girl'.

Defeeted

One morning, the mayor walked into Stephanie's room. She was sitting on her bed, looking glum. "What's the matter?" he asked.

"No-one's outside playing," she answered, sadly. "Stingy won't share his new ball, Pixel's on his computer and Ziggy's taking a nap."

The mayor knew just who could cheer Stephanie up: Sportacus! "Sportacus, let's have a Sportacular Spectacle Day!" he said.

Robbie Rotten didn't like the sound of that. "Maybe my Fleet-Feet Crazer-Maker 6000 will come in handy," he sneered, looking through his periscope.

As Sportacus was on his way to practise a stunt for the Sportacular Spectacle, a salesman appeared. "Your boots are dirty, my friend!" he said.

Sportacus looked down. His boots *were* dirty! "Here, try these," said the salesman, handing him a new pair of boots.

Later that day, everyone gathered for the Sportacular Spectacle. "Sportacus is going to do a sportacular football stunt!" said Ziggy, excitedly.

"I hope my stunt goes well," said Sportacus. "Don't worry," said Stephanie, "you'll do just fine!"

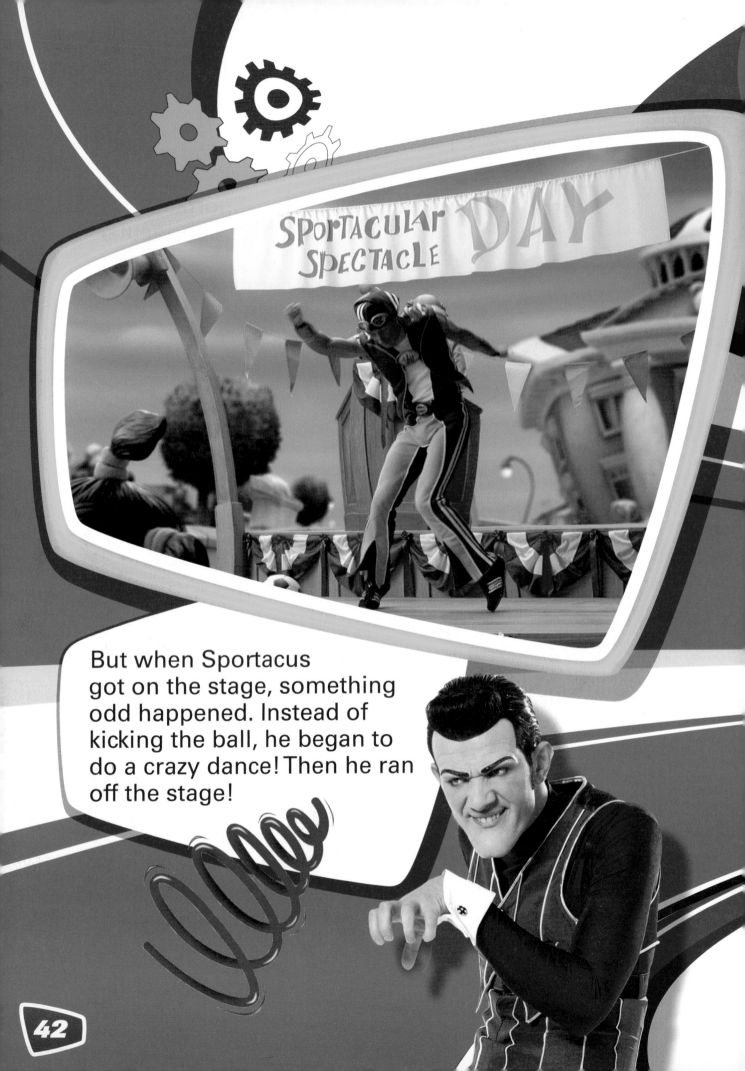

But when Sportacus got on the stage, something odd happened. Instead of kicking the ball, he began to do a crazy dance! Then he ran off the stage!

"Something must be wrong!" said Stephanie. She and the kids rushed to find Sportacus. They found him struggling to keep his feet still.

"Something's wrong with my feet!" he said. "There must be something we can do," said Stephanie. "I know – try walking on your hands!"

Meanwhile, Robbie Rotten was now onstage. "I am your new hero, Lazycus!" he announced. "You must all love ME now."

Just then, there was a shout from the crowd. "Sportacus is back – he's walking on his hands!" cried Stephanie.

Everyone cheered. "That's a great stunt, Sportacus!" they shouted. "Now Lazycus must do a stunt. Do the splits!"

But when Robbie tried to do the splits, his tights ripped! As Robbie shuffled offstage, everyone agreed it was the best Sportacular Spectacle ever!

Lazy Puzzles

Which trail of coins will lead Stingy to his beloved piggy bank?

1

2

3

Write it in!

Two of these computer shapes are exactly the same. Which ones are they?

a

b

c

d

Write it in!

Missing Melody

There are 15 musical notes hidden in this picture. Can you find them all?

Answers on page 68

Let's Dance

Dancing is such good fun! You can do it alone or with your friends. Put on your favourite lively music, and try out some of these steps. Let's go!

1 Bend to one side and turn your palms to the sky.

2 Throw your right arm and leg sideways, and your left arm up.

48

3

Turn to the left and curve your whole body backwards.

4

Finally, jump high in the air and bring up your knees. Great!

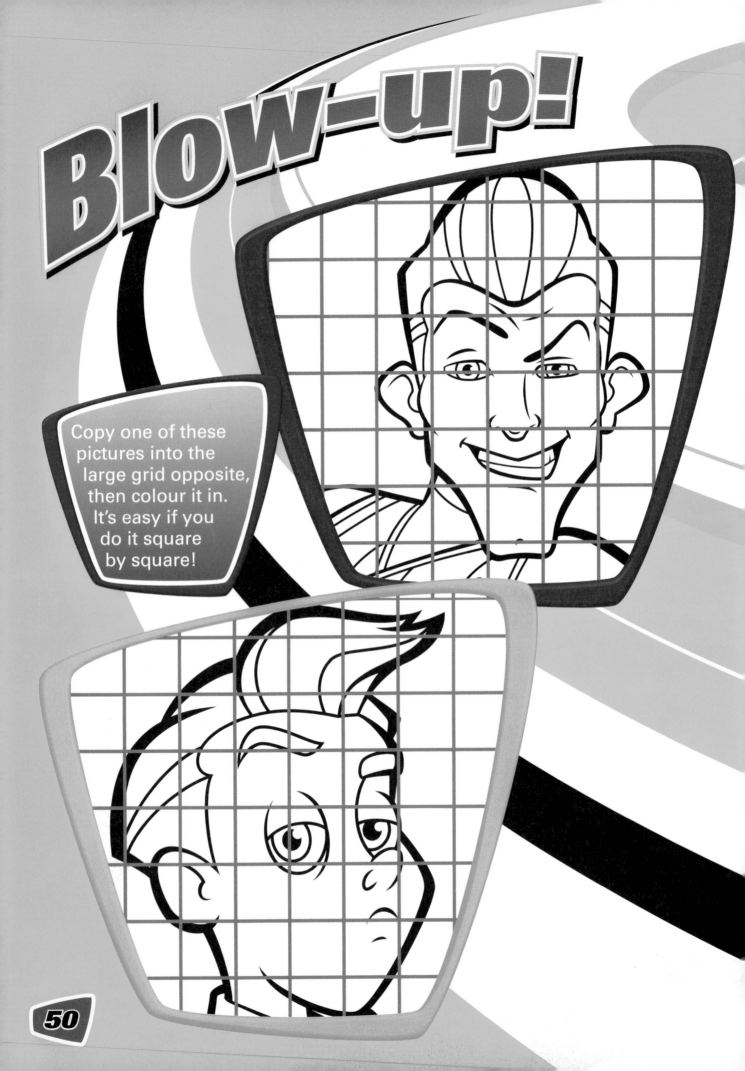

Rotten Potion

Robbie Rotten is cooking up a diabolical potion that will make everyone in LazyTown as lazy as he is! Which funnel is connected to which beaker? Write in the answers at the bottom.

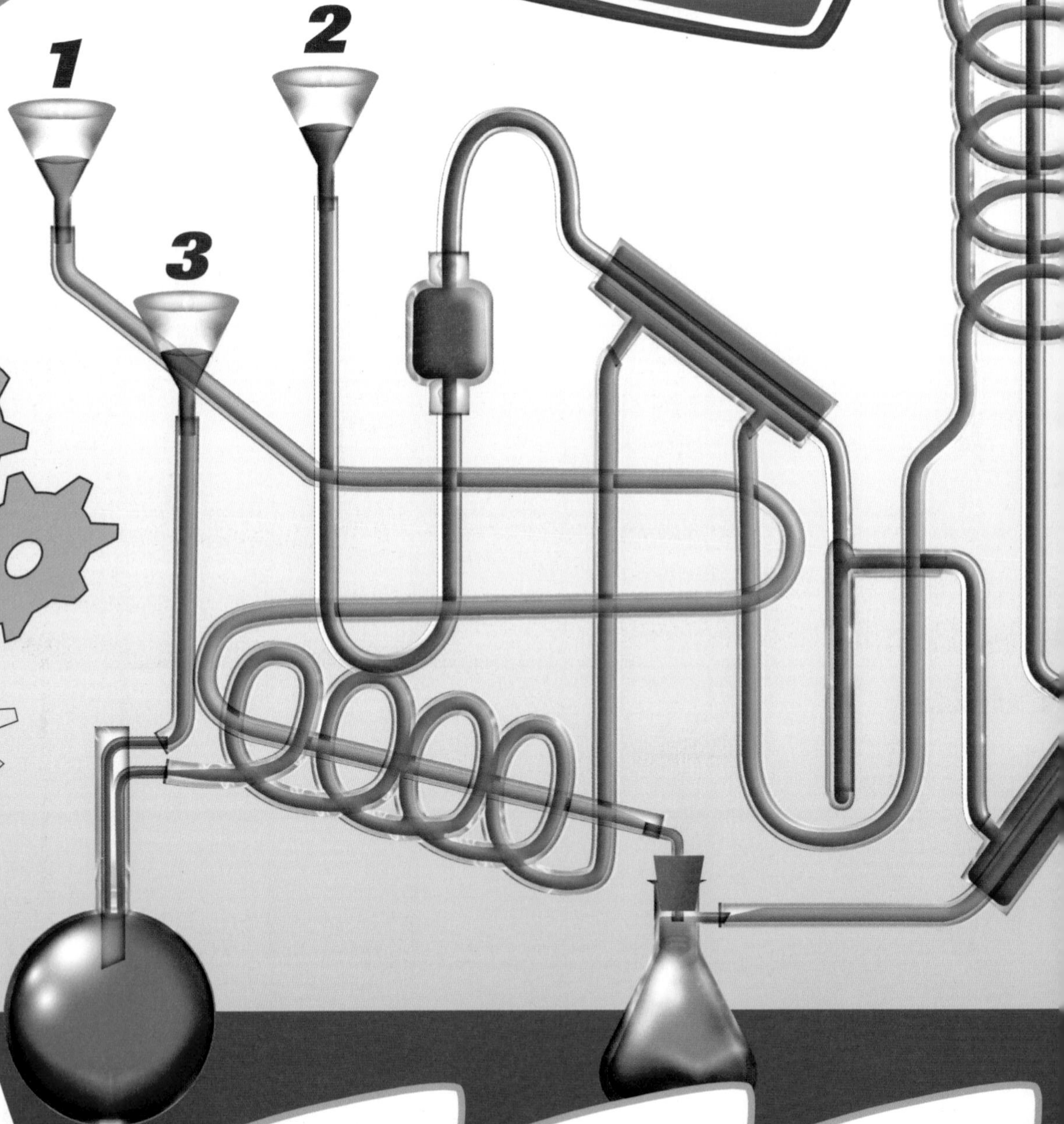

1

2

3

1=

2=

3=

52

Robbie's tip

Take care to follow the colours as you go!

a   b   c

53

The Haunted Castle

One morning, the LazyTown kids were playing with a wagon. "Wheeeeeeeee!" cried Ziggy, as he hurtled downhill holding an ice cream.

Luckily, Sportacus caught him just before he hit Bessie's clean sheets. "Oh, my!" said the mayor. "You kids should really play somewhere else."

"But where, uncle?" asked Stephanie. "You can play in Lazy Park!" he answered. "Just don't go near the Haunted Castle."

Robbie Rotten was not happy. "I can't have kids in my favourite park!" he grumbled. "I'll have to scare them off somehow."

After a day spent playing in the park, Trixie had an idea. "Let's go and explore the Haunted Castle!" she said.

"But the mayor said not to!" whimpered Ziggy. "You wait here, Ziggy," said Stephanie. "We'll be back in five minutes, I promise."

But as the kids stepped inside the castle, the door slammed shut behind them. They tried to open it, but it was stuck. They were trapped!

Meanwhile, Robbie had taken one of Bessie's sheets, and transformed himself into a ghost. "Woooooooo!" he moaned.

Alone in the park, Ziggy found himself face to face with Robbie dressed as a ghost. "Trixie, is that you trying to scare me?" he asked, bravely.

Meanwhile, the kids had climbed to the top of the tower. "Ziggy, look out!" they cried. "A ghost! Run!"

Ziggy looked up. "But if Trixie's up there ... this must be a real ghost!" screamed Ziggy, as he ran away, closely followed by the moaning ghost.

Sportacus heard the kids screaming. "Hold on kids, I'm coming!" he shouted, as he rushed to help them.

Sportacus kicked the castle door down, and freed the kids. When the ghost saw Sportacus, it stopped chasing Ziggy and ran away.

But it got tangled up in Bessie's washing line. As Robbie fell out of his disguise, everyone realised they'd been tricked!

"You were very brave, Ziggy!" said Sportacus. "And we're so sorry we left you alone," said the other kids.

Back in his lair, a weird 'woo woo' noise was scaring Robbie. "Lucky I don't believe in g-g-ghosts!" he squealed. He didn't know it was only an owl!

61

Pick a Pose

Which 3 cards show the same picture of Stephanie? Write their numbers in the boxes below.

Write it in!

Answers on page 68

Say Cheese!

Trixie has been taking photos of LazyTown. But she hasn't quite got to grips with her new camera. Can you tell who (or what) her photos are of?

a

b

c

d

e

f

Missing Links

There are some things missing from this LazyTown picture. How will you finish it off? Don't forget to colour it in!

Ziggy's enormous lollipop needs a pattern ...

What sport is Sportacus playing?

64

Draw something on Pixel's computer screen.

Give Robbie Rotten a cunning disguise!

Draw some sports candy on Stephanie's plate!

65

The Big Quiz

So you think you know LazyTown? Then put your knowledge to the test with this quiz!

Fill in the Gaps

A nice easy round to start with!

1 _____is always trying to get rid of Sportacus.

2 Mayor Meanswell's niece is _____

3 Ziggy's hero is _____

4 Bessie Busybody's secret admirer is _____

5 _____ wants to have more stuff than all his friends.

Gift Time

Who are these presents for? The colours are a clue!

6

7

8

9

10

In a Spin!

Can you work out who's in these twisted pictures?

11

12

13

14

15

Who Said That?

Who do you think might have said these things?

16 'Mmm, Choco-Sugar-Yummies!'

17 'It's all mine!'

18 'I'm a master of disguise!'

19 'Let's see what my computer says I should do!'

20 'There's always a way!'

Check the answers on page 68 and write your score here:

Write it in!

/20

Answers

Page 16-17 **Shadow d matches Stephanie's picture. The path to the carrot is number 3.**

Page 22-23

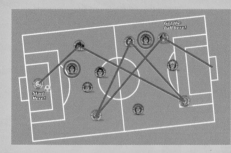

Page 32-33

Page 34-35 **Stephanie is doing the tango, Ziggy is doing the waltz, Stingy is doing the foxtrot and Trixie is doing ballet.**

Page 46-47 **Coin trail number 2 leads to Stingy's piggy bank.**

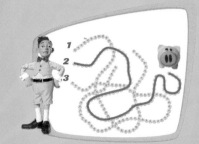

Computer shapes a and d are the same as each other.

Page 52-53 **Pipe number 1 leads to bottle a, pipe number 2 leads to bottle c and pipe number 3 leads to bottle b.**

Page 62-63 **The picture that appears 3 times is on cards 8, 10 and 13.**

**The people and things in Trixie's photos are
a = Stephanie
b = the airship
c = Ziggy
d = Robbie Rotten
e = Bessie Busybody
f = Sportacus.**

Page 66-67 **The missing names are; 1 Robbie Rotten, 2 Stephanie, 3 Sportacus, 4 Mayor Meanswell, 5 Stingy.**

**The presents are for;
6 Robbie Rotten,
7 Sportacus, 8 Trixie,
9 Mayor Meanswell,
10 Stephanie.**

**The twisted pictures are;
11 Sportacus, 12 Trixie,
13 Bessie Busybody,
14 Mayor Meanswell,
15 Robbie Rotten.**

The phrases were said by: 16 Ziggy, 17 Stingy, 18 Robbie Rotten, 19 Pixel, 20 Stephanie.

Spot the Difference

These two covers may look the same, but there are changes in the right hand cover. Tick a box each time you find a difference.

2   3   4   5   6

For **more** fun activities and games, look out for **LazyTown Magazine!** There's a fantastic **free gift** with every issue, and if you **subscribe** now you **save 25%** on the cover price, that's **17 issues for just £25.50.**

To subscribe go to www.titantots.com or call ☎ 0844 322 1249 quoting the promo code **annual08**

Out NOW!

Answers: 1. Stephanie's dress has changed colour. 2. Football has purple patches. 3. Flower near top right corner changed to blue. 4. "Playing indoors!" changed to purple. 5. Robbie Rotten has changed direction. 6. Top banner has changed colour.